P9-DUE-510

# MOSQUITOES CAN'T BITE NINJAS

JORDAN P. NOVAK

**BLOOMSBURY**
NEW YORK  LONDON  OXFORD  NEW DELHI  SYDNEY

WITHDRAWN

# Mosquitoes bite all kinds of people....

For Sally . . . HIYA!

Copyright © 2017 by Jordan P. Novak
All rights reserved. No part of this book may be reproduced or transmitted in any form
or by any means, electronic or mechanical, including photocopying, recording, or by any
information storage and retrieval system, without permission in writing from the publisher.

First published in the United States of America in March 2017
by Bloomsbury Children's Books
www.bloomsbury.com

Bloomsbury is a registered trademark of Bloomsbury Publishing Plc

For information about permission to reproduce selections from this book, write to
Permissions, Bloomsbury Children's Books, 1385 Broadway, New York, New York 10018
Bloomsbury books may be purchased for business or promotional use. For information on bulk purchases please contact
Macmillan Corporate and Premium Sales Department at specialmarkets@macmillan.com

Library of Congress Cataloging-in-Publication Data
Names: Novak, Jordan P., author, illustrator.
Title: Mosquitoes can't bite ninjas / by Jordan P. Novak ; illustrated by Jordan P. Novak.
Other titles: Mosquitoes cannot bite ninjas
Description: New York : Bloomsbury, 2017.
Summary: Mosquitoes are sneaky and quick and can bite all kinds of other people, but they are no match for a ninja.
Identifiers: LCCN 2016008627 (print) | LCCN 2016015787 (e-book)
ISBN 978-1-68119-215-4 (hardcover) • ISBN 978-1-68119-213-0 (e-book) • ISBN 978-1-68119-214-7 (e-PDF)
Subjects: | CYAC: Mosquitoes—Fiction. | Ninja—Fiction. | Humorous stories.
Classification: LCC PZ7.1.N68 Mos 2017 (print) | LCC PZ7.1.N68 (e-book) | DDC[E]—dc23
LC record available at https://lccn.loc.gov/2016008627

Art created with ink drawings rendered and colored digitally
Typeset in Aram ITC Std
Book design by Colleen Andrews
Printed in China by Leo Paper Products, Heshan, Guangdong
2 4 6 8 10 9 7 5 3 1

All papers used by Bloomsbury Publishing, Inc., are natural, recyclable products
made from wood grown in well-managed forests. The manufacturing processes
conform to the environmental regulations of the country of origin.

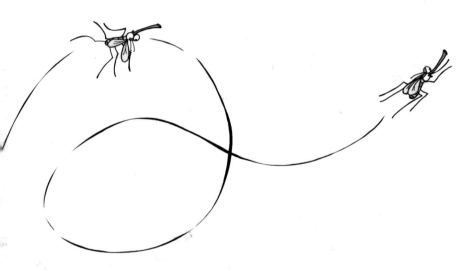

Swimmers.

Chefs.

Old ladies with blue hair.

They even bite babies!

But, as hard as they try, mosquitoes can never bite . . .

... ninjas.

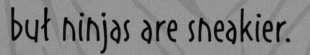

but ninjas are sneakier.

Mosquitoes are quick...

but ninjas are quicker.

Mosquitoes try...

and try...

and try...

for a ninja.

Ninjas don't bite people.

They learn not to when they're baby ninjas.

But every once in a while,

when a ninja is very hungry,

and he isn't paying attention to his sandwich . . .

and a mosquito
gets stuck in
the jelly,

a ninja can bite . . .

a mosquito.

31901060458157